Benito Juarez

66 *I am an Indian and I do not forget my own people.* **99**

Benito Juárez

In 1806 Benito Juárez was born in a village in Mexico. His parents were Zapotec Indians. They died by the time Benito was three years old.

Mexican Indians grinding corn and shaping tortillas

Benito lived with his grandfather and then his uncle. As Benito grew, his days were spent taking care of his uncle's sheep.

A couple working the land in Oaxaca today

In those times Mexico was ruled by Spain.
Like most people in Benito's village, Benito spoke
only Zapotec. He wanted to learn how to speak
and write Spanish.

In Benito's time, priests often taught the
Mexican Indian children to read Spanish.

When Benito was twelve years old, he left his village. He walked about forty miles to the city of Oaxaca. There he stayed in the home where his older sister was living and working.

This church in Oaxaca was built in the 1500s. It is still standing today.

Benito found a job as a houseboy for a very rich man. The man liked Benito and helped him get into school.

Benito studied law at the Institute of Arts and Sciences.

As he grew, Benito saw how the poor were treated differently than the rich. He knew this wasn't fair. He studied to become a lawyer so he could defend the rights of the poor people.

A house in Oaxaca today

By the time Benito finished school, Mexico had won its independence from Spain. The people in the new government still were not fair to many Mexicans. Juárez worked hard to change that.

Benito Juárez

Juárez and Santa Anna fought each other for control of the Mexican government after it won its independence from Spain.

Antonio Santa Anna

Benito Juárez became governor of the state of Oaxaca.
He built schools and roads. The poor loved him
but the rich did not. Juárez was even forced to
leave Mexico, but he returned.

Oaxaca today

9

JUAREZ

Juárez became a powerful lawmaker. One of his laws, called the Juárez Law, said that all Mexicans were equal. Many of his ideas were written into the Constitution of 1857.

The constitution brought reforms to Mexico.

Benito Juárez became president in 1858. Armies in Mexico were fighting each other, but President Juárez led his army to victory.

After many struggles, President Juárez returned to Mexico City in triumph.

President Juárez was welcomed to the palace.

Benito Juárez died in his fourth term as president.
To this day, Mexicans honor him as a great hero.

Monuments to honor Benito Juárez, in Mexico City (above) and in Oaxaca (left)

Let's Explore!

Benito Juárez was born in a village near Oaxaca.
As president, he lived in Mexico City. Point out
Mexico City on the map. Tell which direction
Mexico City is from Oaxaca.

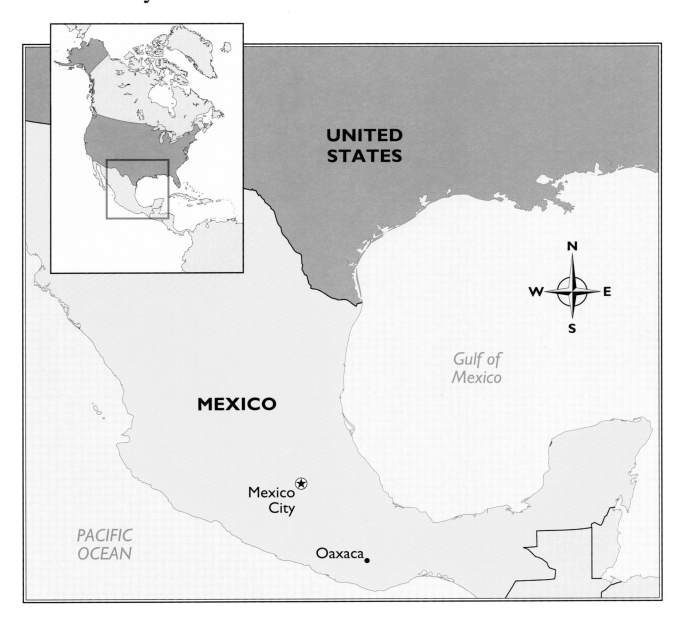

What Do You Think?

Spanish Words

Benito learned Spanish when he was twelve years old. Learn two words in Spanish, such as *hello* and *good-bye*. Use the words with a friend.

Man of the People

Benito Juárez went to Oaxaca when he was twelve years old. He hardly spoke Spanish. Write about how you felt on your first day in school or in a new place.

Juárez Monument

Learning How

Benito wanted to learn how to speak Spanish. What would you like to learn to do? Draw a picture of yourself doing that.

CINCO DE MAYO

On the morning of May 5, 1862, the Mexican army beat the French army at the city of Puebla. Eventually, the Mexicans, under the leadership of Benito Juárez, won their freedom. Every year on May 5th, many Mexicans and Mexican Americans celebrate *Cinco de Mayo*.

Key Events

1806   Born in the state of Oaxaca, Mexico

1818   Went to city of Oaxaca to study

1828   Went to college

1831   Started practicing law in Oaxaca

1843   Married Margarita Maza

1847   Elected governor of the state of Oaxaca

1855   Became Minister of Justice

1858   Became president of Mexico

1872   Died in Mexico City

In 1972, Mexico's ambassador presented a
portrait of Benito Juárez to the librarian
of the Library of Congress.